Jakers!

Piggley Helps Out

Adapted by Alison Inches
Images by Entara

SIMON AND SCHUSTER

Jakers!

Hello there, my name
is Granda Piggley
and I would like to tell
you a story from when
I was growing up.

Gather round and
I'll tell you all about
my adventures down
on Raloo Farm, with
my two best friends,
Ferny and Dannan.

Jakers! what fun
we used to have…

is sad.

MISS NANNY

Her is lost!

CAT

"We can find your !"

CAT

say , , and .

PIGGLEY   FERNY   DANNAN

"Thank you," says .

MISS NANNY

"If you can find my ,

CAT

I will give you some ."

SWEETS

"Jakers!" says .

PIGGLEY

"We **love** !"

SWEETS

C13

"Tell us about your  LoLo,"
CAT

said .
DANNAN

"My  is white,"
CAT

said  .
MISS NANNY

"My  loves  rides,
CAT CAR

, and  .
BASKETS FISH

My  is the best
CAT CAT

in the  ."
WORLD

, , and

PIGGLEY   FERNY   DANNAN

look for the

CAT

all day long.

 ,
PIGGLEY

 ,
FERNY

and are
DANNAN

about to give up when . . .

"Look!" said .
DANNAN

"I see the !"
CAT

The is next to a .
CAT   PLANT

PIGGLEY   FERNY   , and   DANNAN

put the in their .

CAT   WAGON

"  will be so happy!"

MISS NANNY

said  .

PIGGLEY

But it is not 's !

MISS NANNY   CAT

"My is all white,"

CAT

said .

MISS NANNY

MISS NANNY gives PIGGLEY , FERNY ,

and DANNAN some SWEETS for

trying.

"  is so sad," said .

MISS NANNY   DANNAN

"How can we enjoy our

?" asks .

SWEETS   FERNY

"We **must** find her !"

CAT

said .

PIGGLEY

"What do we know about 's ?" asks .

MISS NANNY   CAT   DANNAN

" 's is all white,"

MISS NANNY   CAT

said 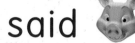.

PIGGLEY

"She loves rides, ,

CAR   BASKETS

and  ," said . " And

FISH   FERNY

she is the best in the ."

CAT   WORLD

"I know!" cries .

DANNAN

"The is in the   !"

CAT   FISH   VAN

" 's is here!"

MISS NANNY   CAT

said .

PIGGLEY

"Now we can take the  home!"

CAT

"Not so fast!"

Who said that? It is !

HECTOR

"Give me the !" said .

CAT   HECTOR

We will not give you 's ," cries .

MISS NANNY   CAT   PIGGLEY

But we will give you our ."

SWEETS

 takes the .

HECTOR   SWEETS

, , and

PIGGLEY   FERNY   DANNAN

take the back to .

CAT   MISS NANNY

"My !" said .

CAT   MISS NANNY

"I missed you so much!"

 thanks 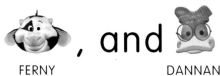,

MISS NANNY   PIGGLEY

, and 

FERNY   DANNAN

for their help.

"We made happy!"

MISS NANNY

said .

PIGGLEY

"And that is better than

all the in the !"

SWEETS   WORLD